LET'S GET SLEEPY!

by TONY CLIFF

{Imprint}
MAKE YOUR MARK
NEW YORK

Let's all get up early! No more sleeping late!
Today's a new chance to achieve something great!

Look who's up early. Good morning, hello.

But what happened to Sleepy? Where did he go?

Mom must mean wee Sleepy, the Prince of the Night,
The Master of Dreams, and the King of Moonlight.
But where is he now? Where could Sleepy be?
Not here, not around us. He's run away, free!

But we'll get him again. We'll catch us that mouse.

    Let's get on our shoes,

        Let's get out of the house and . . .

Our neighborhood block! Is this where he'll be?

We'll search and we'll seek and ask friends that we meet.

Come look downtown with us!

Let's climb up a tree and survey the whole street.

Let's not close our eyes till our search is complete.

We can get on our bikes so we cover more ground.

Where can that mouse be? Where could he be found?

A weekend parade! Is this where he'll be?
We'll search and we'll seek and ask friends that we meet.

Maybe he's down
by the water?

Let's ride on a float and let's play in the band.

We can ask if the mayor might lend us a hand.

Let's go mix with the crowd; let's start asking around.

Where can that mouse be? Where could he be found?

Sunny Sands Beach! Is this where he'll be?

We'll search and we'll seek and ask friends that we meet.

You should try the mountaintops.

Let's look in the surf and let's scour the shore.

We'll turn over rocks till we can't anymore.

Let's build him a castle set right by the sea.

Where can he be found? Where could that mouse be?

MAX'S

The peaks of Mount Snow! Is this where he'll be?
We'll search and we'll seek and ask friends that we meet.

Let's roll up a snowman and build a snow fort.
Cavort with our friends in some wintery sport.
Is Sleepy a mouse who might know how to ski?
Where can he be found? Where could that mouse be?

LET'S

Ol' Tropical Swamp! Is this where he'll be?

We'll search and we'll seek and ask friends that we meet.

But have you tried looking underground?

Let's check out those bugs—they're the size of a bus!

Let's try to scare off the T. rex watching us.

There are traces of Sleepy, footprints all around.

Where can that mouse be? Where could he be found?

'The Wonder Slug Caves! Is this where he'll be?
We'll search and we'll seek and ask friends that we meet.

There's one last place you could look . . .

Let's unearth some gems and let's search in the dark.

We can see by the light of the glowworms' glow marks.

The ground is the ceiling! The ceiling's the ground!

Where can that mouse be? Where could he be found?

The moon! Yes, the moon! Is this where he'll be?

We'll search and we'll seek and ask friends that we meet.

Let's play a few games and kick up some moondust.

Let's trust we'll find clues in the soft lunar crust.

I'm tired! All day we've been running around.

Where can that mouse be? Where could he be found?

Let's

get Sleepy.

How was your day? Tell me, what did you do?

Did you capture the mouse who you thought escaped you?

I didn't! We couldn't! We tried, but did not.

I didn't get Sleepy. He couldn't be caught.

I got some new friends, got to lead a parade.

I got sand down my shorts and got lost in a cave.

I got snow in my socks, got to ride a T. rex.

I got shoes full of moondust, full of little moon specks.

But! I did not
            get
                  Sleepy.

What a wonderful day! What adventures you've led.

You've got so many memories to take to your bed.

Let's think about all the new places you've been.

Let's close up our eyes on the sights that we've seen.

Let's put our heads down

and pull up the sheets,

and let's . . .

get . . .

Sleepy.

[Imprint]
A part of Macmillan Publishing Group, LLC
120 Broadway, New York, NY 10271

ABOUT THIS BOOK
The artwork for this book was produced using a combination of traditional and digital
techniques, primarily 2B pencil on copier paper. The text was set in Adobe Caslon, and
the display type is hand-lettered. The book was edited by Erin Stein and art directed
by Natalie C. Sousa. The production was supervised by Raymond Ernesto Colón, and the
production editor was Hayley Jozwiak.

Library of Congress Control Number: 2019949742
ISBN 978-1-250-30784-2 (hardcover)

Our books may be purchased in bulk for promotional, educational, or business use. Please
contact your local bookseller or the Macmillan Corporate and Premium Sales Department at
(800) 221-7945 ext. 5442 or by email at MacmillanSpecialMarkets@macmillan.com.
Imprint logo designed by Amanda Spielman
First edition, 2020
10 9 8 7 6 5 4 3 2 1
mackids.com